BRANDON THE BULLY
Meets
NINA-NO MORE

Written by Phyllis D. Brooks

Illustrations by Blueberry Illustrations

ISBN 978-1-936634-71-2

Printed in USA by 48HrBooks

Blueberry illustrations is known for Children book illustrations and has worked with many Authors's who had a dream to get published. With their in house illustrators one feel at ease and one can see their imagination coming to life on paper.
Website: www.bluberryillustrations.com

To Davia, my entire family, circle of friends, and kids being bullied everywhere!

Brandon the Bully wakes up
mad every day.
He blames everyone with
bad things to say.

He pushes and pulls on kids
smaller than him.
He makes them cry,
makes their days feel grim.

On the way home from school
he does it again,
hitting Allie and Jock
and picking on Ben.

He walks towards his house
and sees his mom outside.
He picks up the pace
and begins to smile.

His mom hugs him tight without
a clue in the world,
That her precious boy Brandon
picks on boys and girls.

As he walks with his mom,
she speaks in his ear,
"I have to work late,"
for the tenth time this year.

Deep down inside
Brandon gets sad.
Maybe if she was home,
he wouldn't be bad.
So he goes to his room,
when she leaves him alone.
With his teenage sister,
who lives on her phone.

Sometimes Brandon feels
like no one cares,
So he thinks to himself,
"Everyone beware.
If I feel this bad then
they should too.
I'll make them feel
sad just like I do."

The next day at school
as recess begins,
Brandon the Bully
summons the gang in.
They all come over to
where Brandon stands,
Corey, Clinton, Tyler, and Dan.

They stand there and
watch as Brandon begins,
to look for a target
to pick on again.
He trips a young kid and
then takes his lunch.
He then makes him cry with
one single punch.

When recess ends and gym class begins,
Brandon the Bully walks in with a grin.
Most of the kids are wishing that maybe,
Brandon the Bully would stop with the hazing.

A day with no teasing,
no hitting, or kicking,
but a day with just laughing
and playing and singing.
No one ever thought
that the bullying would end,
Until a surprise blows
in like the wind!

She walks towards the crowd
where students are gathered.
She pushes her way through
And asks, "What's the matter?"

"Brandon the Bully hit me," said Chris,
"He yelled in my face and showed me his fists.
He knocked me over and I fell to the floor,"
"This has to stop!" said Nina-No More.

Nina stands firm with Destiny do-Good,
Her BFF from her neighborhood.
The teachers are trying to quiet the crowd,
It works for a moment but then the
teachers get loud!

Nina said "Chris get u
and stand tall.
This whole situation
affects us all.
Brandon the Bully is
not really bad,
I bet deep down,
he's just really sad."

"I once knew a bully her name was Brianna,
She bothered me daily and I would tell my mama.
My mama said "baby don't run and be scared,
Keep telling an adult they can
help you be prepared."

So I told the teacher who told Brianna's parents,
Who had no idea of their daughter's bad manners.
Soon things got better and the bullying stopped,
Brianna was nicer and her
bad habits were dropped."

When Brandon approaches Nina-no More,
she holds up her hand and he stumps the floor!
Brandon tries to push her off to the side,
As Nina pushes back her friends look with pride.
Brandon the Bully is stunned and surprised.
A girl stands up to him, and she's half his size.

As Nina stands strong with no intentions of moving,
Brandon the Bully yells, "What are you doing?"
He looks really mad as he crumbles his fists.
The sweat from his face no one could miss.
But Nina-no More does not move an inch,
She says "let me help you, it's a cinch!"
She said "Brandon this pushing
and pulling's not pleasing,
and all of the hitting, and kicking and teasing."

"I believe that deep down
you're really quite sweet,
with tons of good thoughts from
your head to your feet.
Your screams for attention make quite a din,
and tells me that you need the plan, BEGIN!
It was taught to me by my mom and dad,
As a tool to use when I feel sad.
BEGIN will help you deal with your feelings.
You'll be much happier and
your friends will be reeling!"

Brandon is stunned and softens his face,
while this tiny sized girl strengthens her case.
He loosens his hands from the fists they are in,
and listens as Nina speaks of BEGIN.
"It's really quite simple there are only five rules.
The first one's the best and starts with you!"

The gym is silent as everyone listens,
even the teachers do not want to miss it.
Nina says "B", is for believe in yourself,
and don't get discouraged from anyone else.
This is the first thing that you have to do.
Now let's move on to rule number two!"

"E" is to empower yourself
and stand tall.
Share smiles with others,
get up if you fall.
Empowerment means
finding the tools that you need,
to help you stay positive
and succeed.
They should be tools that make
you feel good,
like helping a neighbor in your neighborhood."

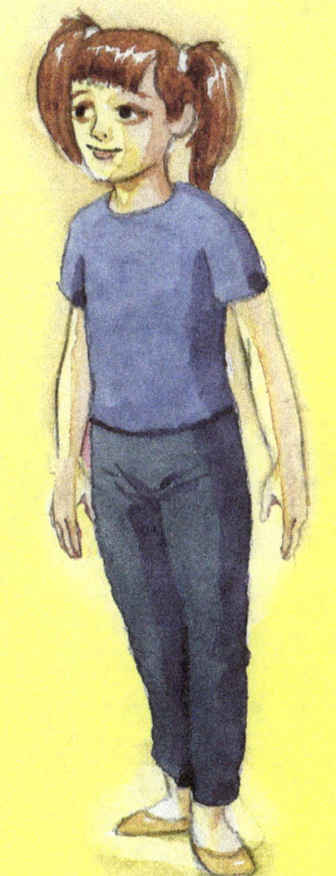

"Now that we've listened to rule number two,
The third rule will tell you what you need to do.
G is for get up," Said Nina, "on your feet,
It's time to get moving because now you believe!
You don't have to bully and pretend
that you're bad.
Get up and show others you're no longer mad.
Helping others will make you feel good inside.
It'll brighten your spirit and brighten your smile.
The teachers will help you and so will your friends.
Your parents and sister will help with BEGIN!"

"The next is I for initiate.
Which means speak up, stand up, don't wait!
"What else does this mean?" a kid yells real loud.
"E-NI-SHE-ATE," another yells from the crowd.

Destiny-do Good steps forward with care,
She walks through the crowd
giving Brandon a glare.
"Initiate means start something, get moving
Like the ease of a ship when it
finally starts cruising.

You're the Captain aboard so you lead the way,
Take charge of your dreams, today is your day!"
A circle is formed with the kids and the teachers,
Everyone is coming down from the bleachers.

Brandon the Bully is now in the middle,
because of this girl who once seemed so little.
But not anymore, and what a surprise!
Now finally Nina shouts, "Rule number five!"

"Never give up!
You have what it takes!
We all have the same
chance to be great!
Being bullied makes kids
feel bad inside,
It happened to me
because of my size!

But now I am happy I try to help others,
So they won't feel sad, scarred or worried."
"Thank you for Begin and helping others,"
Said one of the teachers, "Yes!" said another!

Brandon the Bully gives
Nina no More,
the biggest hug ever
and runs towards the door.
He turns to the crowd
and flashes a big grin,
"No more Bullying for me,
 I now have BEGIN!"

ABOUT THE AUTHOR

Phyllis Brooks is a native of South Carolina. She holds a Bachelors of Arts in English/Communications from Columbia College and a Master of Arts in the field of Speech Language Pathology from SC State University. She currently resides in Charlotte NC and is employed as a Speech Pathologist in an educational setting as well as medical settings. She published her first book, "Let Me BE Your Coach" in 2010, a five step plan for youth to stay motivated, reach goals, and never give up on their dreams based on her own trials and accomplishments and those of other successful people. She is increasing her presence in the realm of Motivational Speaking with a focus on adolescents and young adults to motivate them to never give up on their goals. She has spoken to more than 2000 kids, teachers and adults to extend her message of positive thinking to reach goals based on her BEGIN program. She is a member of the American Speech-Language and Hearing Association, Biltmore Who's Who of America, National Association of Professional Women, Women Who Care Coalition, and National Association of Strength and Conditioning for Fitness. Her resume also consists of being a graduate of Barbizon Modeling agency and has performed in several local commercials and plays. Her additional passions of writing and motivating others include, fitness, traveling, and spending time with her fifteen year old daughter. She has a certification in personal training and has been featured on the cover of the first addition of a local style magazine as a role-model for women. She also continues to persue her dream of acting.

9 781936 634712